THE EVENT

DANIEL GRANT

PART 7

ISBN-13: 978-1-948297-22-6

DALLENT

VERY *ELABORATE* ROLEPLAYING, AND *SO VERY SEXY!*

GRACE HAS TO BE THE *HOTTEST* WOMAN I'VE *EVER* MET!

BUT -- SHE HAS A *GIRLFRIEND* AND PROBABLY DOESN'T EVEN *LIKE* GUYS!

HOPEFULLY, WE'LL *SAVE* THE ELF MAIDEN AND TAKE HER WITH US TO THE *FINAL DOMAIN!*

HECK.

MAYBE *SHE'S AVAILABLE?*

ELFLAND SOUNDS *INTERESTING!*

NO *DOUBT* A BUNCH OF *HORNY* PEOPLE DRESSED UP LIKE *ELVES.*

I JUST *WONDER* WHAT *DARCI* IS UP TO?

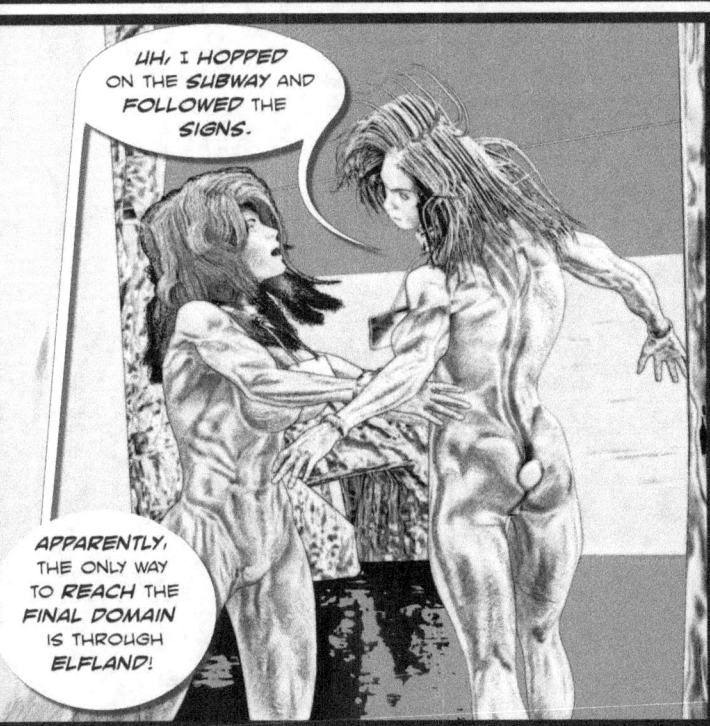